What Is a Neighbo...
Neighbo...

By Jenna Lee Gleisner

SPARKS

Picture Glossary

My neighborhood
is big.

It has a park.

park

My neighborhood
is big.

It has a library.

library

My neighborhood
is big.

It has a school.

school

My neighborhood
is big.

It has a post office.

My neighborhood
is big.

It has a pool.

pool

13

My neighborhood is big.

It has many homes.

homes

Do You Know?

What is this neighborhood spot?

park

library

school

pool

16